Thank You, Grandpa

Thank You, Grandpa

by Lynn Plourde

illustrated by

Jason Cockcroft

Dutton Children's Books ✦ New York

*The author wishes to gratefully acknowledge
that this book was made possible,
in part, by a Barbara Karlin Grant
from the Society of Children's Book Writers and Illustrators.*

CIP Data is available.

Published in the United States 2003 by Dutton Children's Books,
a division of Penguin Putnam Books for Young Readers
345 Hudson Street, New York, New York 10014
www.penguinputnam.com

Designed by Beth Herzog

Printed in Hong Kong
First Edition
1 3 5 7 9 10 8 6 4 2
ISBN 0-525-46992-3

Thank you and good-bye to

Grammy
[ADRIEN AMBROSE, 1908–1969]

Gee
[VIRGINIA BRIDGHAM, 1910–1996]

and Pépère
[LEON PLOURDE SR., 1912–1998]

— L.P.

To Charles Cockcroft,

Arthur Simpson,

Tom Hassal,

and Wilfred "Joe" Wrench

— J.C.

They took their first walks together when the little girl was barely old enough to toddle. Grandfather and granddaughter wobbled along, side by side, hand in hand, smile to smile.

Two steps and "Oooooh!" as they stopped
to pick a dandelion.

Three steps more and "Wheeeee!" as a bird
flew out of the bushes.

Before long, the little girl raced ahead, bubbling with questions.

"What's that, Grandpa?"

"A thirsty bee sipping nectar."

"And that?"

"A sneaky snake playing hide-and-seek with us."

Each walk brought a new discovery.

"Look, Grandpa. That squirrel is waving his tail at us."

Grandpa chuckled, waving back at the squirrel.

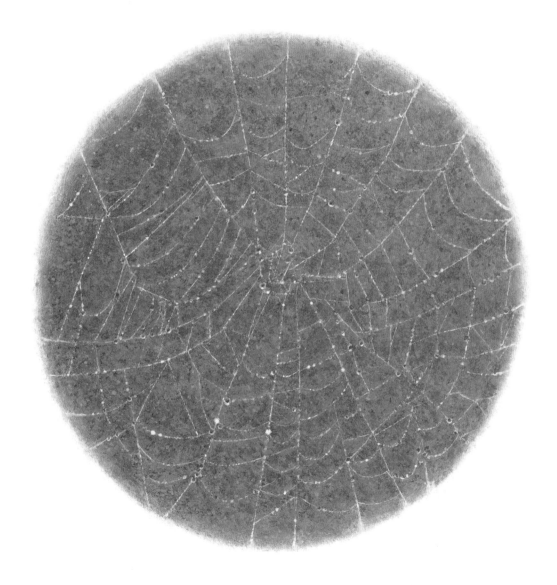

"Over there, Grandpa. That spiderweb is crying."

"Yes, child. Teardrops of dew."

One day, they found a grasshopper lying still.
Too still.

"Grandpa, is it dead?"

"Yes, child, it is."

"What can we do?"

"We can say thank you and good-bye."

They scooped out a hole and gently placed the grasshopper in it.

Grandpa said, "Thank you for your hops, grasshopper. You showed me how to add a bounce to my step. Thank you and good-bye."

Then it was the little girl's turn. "Thank you for always surprising me, grasshopper. You'd hide in the grass and then pop out, like magic. Thank you and good-bye."

Then she sprinkled dirt on top of the grasshopper and patted the dirt into a smooth mound.

Over the years, there were many more "thank you's" and "good-byes."

They found a butterfly on the side of the road, and Grandpa said, "You have traveled far from caterpillar to butterfly. Thank you for showing us how to age with beauty and grace."

The girl added, "Thank you, butterfly, for being a flower with wings."

On a wintry walk, they found a mouse. The
girl said, "Thank you for being brave in such
a big world."

"Yes," Grandpa agreed, covering the mouse with
his wool mitten. "May you be warm at last."

On a moonless night, the girl chased fireflies,
racing from flash to flash. Then she walked over
to her grandfather, suddenly sad.

"Thanks for your quiet fireworks, firefly. You
made the Fourth of July last all summer long."

Grandpa added, "And thank you for brightening our journey into the night."

They took their last walks together when
Grandpa was too old to walk by himself.
Grandfather and granddaughter shuffled along,
side by side, hand in hand, smile to smile.

Until one day the girl walked alone.

Two steps, and she stopped to pick a gone-by dandelion.

Three steps more, and she held the dandelion up
to the sky.

"Thank you, Grandpa, for our walks. You kept me steady when I wasn't so steady. You let me run ahead when I was ready to run ahead. Thank you for sharing spiderweb tears and firefly flashes. But most of all, thank you for teaching me the words I need to say."

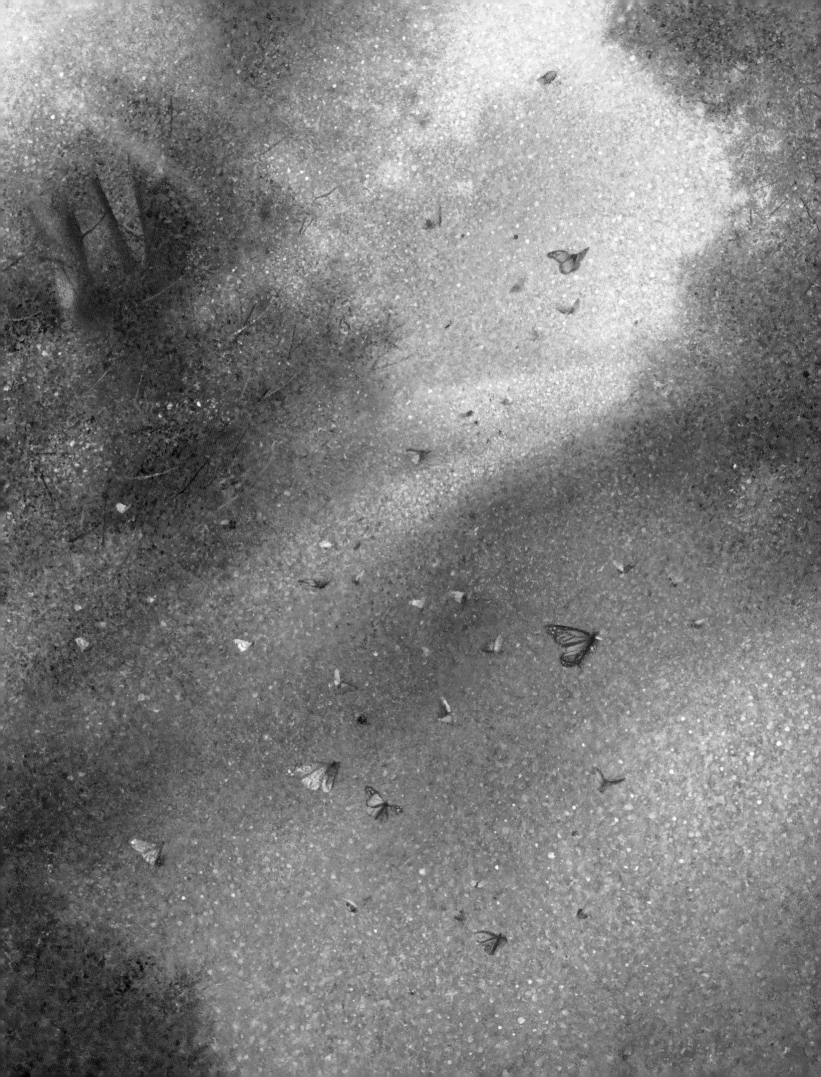

Then the girl blew on the dandelion.

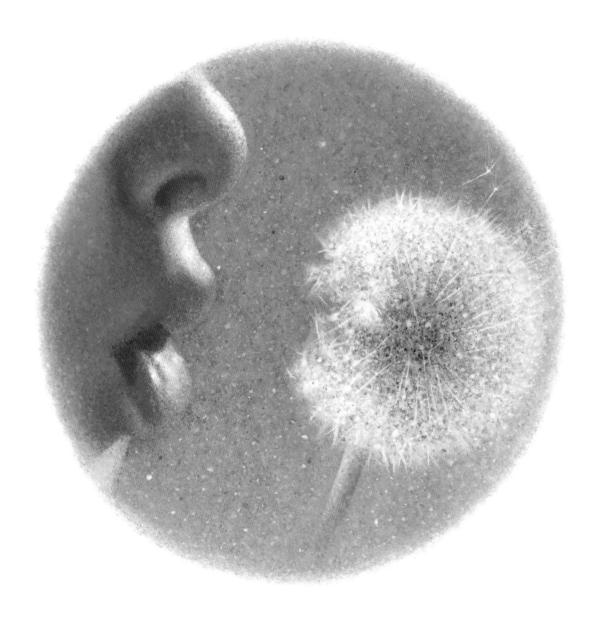

"Grandpa, I love you and I'll miss you. But I will never forget you."

"Thank you and good-bye."